CIP Data is available.

Published in the United States 2000 by Dutton Children's Books,
a division of Penguin Putnam Books for Young Readers
345 Hudson Street, New York, New York 10014
http://www.penguinputnam.com/yreaders/index.htm

Originally published in Great Britain 1999 by Hamish Hamilton Ltd, London
Typography by Richard Amari
Printed in Singapore
First American Edition
ISBN 0-525-46231-7
2 4 6 8 10 9 7 5 3 1

DAISY'S
BABIES

LISA KOPPER

Dutton Children's Books ✦ NEW YORK

Daisy has three puppies: Morris, Dolores, and Little Daisy.

Baby is their friend.

But when Baby wants to play…

Morris doesn't.

When Baby wants to read...

Dolores doesn't.

When Baby wants to hide…

Little Daisy doesn't.

And when Morris, Dolores,
and Little Daisy want to sleep…

Baby doesn't.

Now all the babies want
to watch TV…

but Daisy doesn't!

Daisy wants to smell nice
and look pretty.

Everybody helps.

But when Mommy says,
"Who wants to clean up?"

nobody does.

Then she says,
"Who wants a snack?"

Everybody does!

DATE DUE

		AUG 5 2001
		AUG 2 8 2000
		NOV 0 8 2001
		FEB 2 5 2002
		APR 8 - 2002
		APR 2 0 2002
		MAY 3 0 2002
		SEP 1 8 2003
		DEC 1 - 2003

Discard

GAYLORD   PRINTED IN U.S.A.